AF654158

Arabian Nights
Alibaba and the Forty Thieves

Om KIDZ
An imprint of Om Books International

Once upon a time, in Persia, there lived two brothers- Kasim and Alibaba. While Kasim married the daughter of a rich merchant and ran a luxury shop, Alibaba married a poor woman and sold dry wood in the market.

One fine day, Alibaba was chopping wood when he saw a group of forty thieves on horses galloping towards him. He thought to himself, 'I must hide or they will kill me.' He climbed a tree and watched them ride towards a cave.

One of the men stood in front of the cave and said, 'Open Sesame,' and the cave magically opened. Alibaba was taken aback. After some time, the group emerged from the cave and another one of them said, 'Shut Sesame,' and the cave closed.

Alibaba thought to himself as he watched the thieves go, 'Why don't I try the magic words and enter the cave?' Standing in front of the cave he said, 'Open Sesame,' and watched the cave open. The cave was filled with jewels and riches which the thieves had stolen over the years!

Alibaba went back and told Kasim about the thieves. Kasim wanted to go to the cave and try his luck. But Alibaba warned him about the thieves. He didn't listen and went ahead anyway. He said the magical words and the cave opened to reveal the treasures to him. By now, the thieves were on

their way to the cave. They found Kasim inside the cave, filling bags with gold coins and treasures. They killed him instantly, leaving his body inside.

The next morning, Alibaba went looking for his brother and found his body inside the cave. He thought to himself, 'Oh Kasim, I had warned you!' He took his brother's body back and with the help of Marjenah, Kasim's loyal servant, gave him a burial.

On discovering that the body was missing from the cave, the forty thieves realised that someone knew their secret and decided to track him down. Through one of the villagers at Kasim's burial, the thieves discovered Alibaba!

Then, one day, one of the thieves found Alibaba's house. He put a cross mark on the house so that he could come back with other thieves later. That night, the forty thieves returned to the village. When they came, they found cross marks on all houses!

Smart Marjenah had seen the thief put the cross mark and proceeded to fool them this way. The thieves connived again. This time, their leader showed them jars filled with oil and said, 'I will dress up as an oil merchant and visit Alibaba. You will get inside these jars and when I signal to you by throwing stones, rush out of your jars and attack him.'

The leader visited Alibaba with forty jars, one filled with oil and the other thirty-nine, hiding the other thieves. He asked him for food and Alibaba invited him to dine with them. Marjenah discovered there was no oil in the house. So she thought of taking oil from the jars. As she opened the jar filled with oil, the thief inside the other jar thought it was time to jump out. So he asked in a soft tone, 'Is it time, Master?' thinking it was the leader outside.

Clever Marjenah replied in a manly voice, 'Not yet!' She had realized that the pack of thieves was hiding in the jars. She took the oil from the first jar, heated it and poured it in each jar, killing them one by one. From forty, the thieves were reduced to one.

When the leader threw out some stones as a signal, none of the thieves appeared. He was shocked to discover that they were dead. In anger, he left Alibaba's house and rode away to the forest.

The leader was devastated and decided to take revenge. So he came back to Alibaba's house as a silk merchant. Once more, Marjenah tricked the leader by pulling out the dagger hidden under the leader's silk garment and killing the last thief of the lot.

Alibaba was grateful to Marjenah for saving his life from the thieves and asked her to marry his only son. Alibaba was the only man left with the secret of the cave. He visited it after a year and found all the gold where it was. He finally shared the secret of the cave with his son and everyone lived happily.